★ American Girl®

WellieWishers™

Kendall's Snow Fort

W9-APU-710

Adapted by Meredith Rusu
from the screenplay by Robyn Brown

Scholastic Inc.

ISBN 978-1-338-25432-7

10 9 8 7 6 5 4 3 2 1   18 19 20 21 22

Printed in the U.S.A. 40
First printing 2018

Book design by Carolyn Bull

Animation art direction by Jessica Rogers
and Riley Wilkinson

Scholastic Inc.
557 Broadway, New York, NY 10012

Brrr! It's a cold winter day. Snow covers the ground in the garden.

But the WellieWishers are not cold. They are nice and warm inside their playhouse!

Willa, Ashlyn, and Camille look out the window.

"The animals must be chilly," Camille says. "It's too bad they don't have a cozy playhouse like ours."

That gives Kendall an idea. "We should build a snow fort for the animals!"

"A fort made of snow?" Ashlyn asks. "Wouldn't it be cold?"

"Not if we build it the right way," Kendall says.

She draws a plan. The fort has walls, a door, and even a roof. All made out of snow!

"Kendall, you are a genius!" Ashlyn says.
"Let's do it!" the other WellieWishers shout.

Just then, the wind blows outside. Dark clouds gather. A snowstorm is coming.

"Uh-oh," Kendall says. "Maybe this isn't such a good idea. We might not finish before the storm comes."

"We can do it," Emerson says. "We just have to work super-fast."

"We'll all help," Camille adds.

"I don't know," Kendall says slowly. "Sometimes you guys start projects and don't finish them. I don't want that to happen to our fort."

"We'll get it done. We promise,"
Ashlyn says.

"Come on, Kendall," Willa adds.
"The animals would love it."

Kendall nods. "Okay. Let's do it!"

The WellieWishers get to work.
First, they gather lots of snow.
Then, Kendall shows them how to
shape the walls.
Everything is going great. Until . . .

PLOP!

Snow falls from a tree onto Willa's head.

"Hey!" Willa cries. "Who threw a snowball at me?"

Emerson laughs. "It wasn't me!"

Willa knows Emerson is telling the truth, but she starts a fun snowball fight anyway. Camille and Ashlyn join in.

Kendall is left to work on the fort by herself.
"You guys, you promised you would help until
the fort was finished," she reminds them.
"Oh, right, sorry!" Willa says. "Back to work!"

A little while later, the fort is looking good.

"Bingo-bango!" Kendall says. "We're almost done!"

"Hmmmm," Ashlyn says. "The fort is missing something."

"Yeah, the most important part," Kendall says. "The roof."

"No," Ashlyn replies. "It needs decorations!"

"Like pinecones!" Camille says.

"Ooh! And a snowman out front!" Emerson adds.

The girls start working on their decoration ideas.

"But . . . the roof!" Kendall says. "If the storm comes, the fort won't be strong enough without a roof."

"Don't worry," Willa says. "We'll help you in a few minutes."

"You can trust us!" Ashlyn says.

But Kendall doesn't believe them.
"I did trust you!" she shouts. "You promised you would help and now you're not!"

Suddenly, the wind blows really hard. WHOOSH!

Without a roof, the snow fort collapses!
"See?" Kendall cries. "Now everything
is ruined!" She runs away to another part
of the garden.

Kendall's friends feel bad.

"Kendall's right," Ashlyn says. "We broke our promise. We stopped working before the fort was finished."

"There's only one way to make it up to her," Willa says. "Does anyone know how to build a roof?"

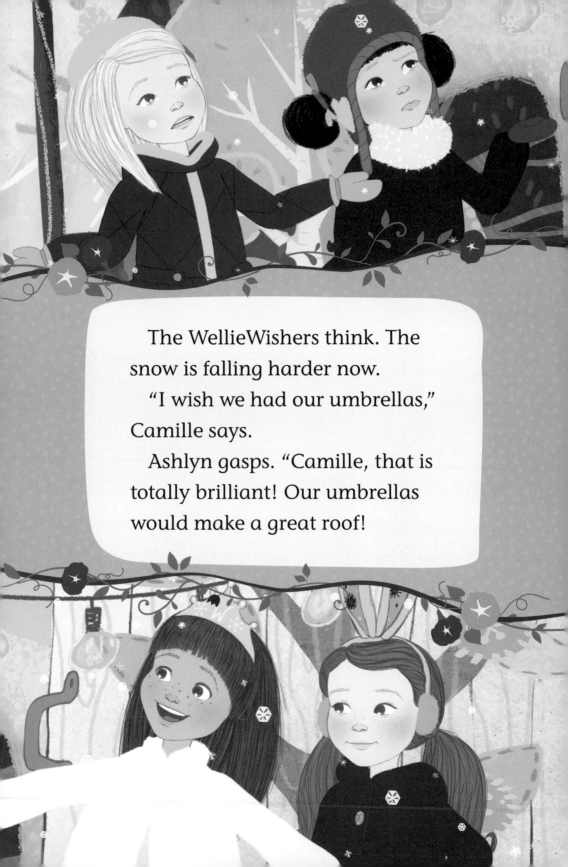

The WellieWishers think. The snow is falling harder now.

"I wish we had our umbrellas," Camille says.

Ashlyn gasps. "Camille, that is totally brilliant! Our umbrellas would make a great roof!

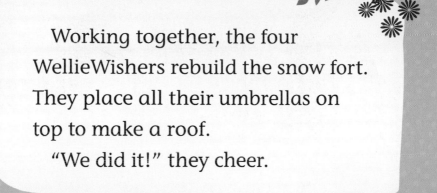

Working together, the four
WellieWishers rebuild the snow fort.
They place all their umbrellas on
top to make a roof.

"We did it!" they cheer.

From the other side of the garden, Kendall hears the cheering. She goes back to the playhouse.

"Not bad," she tells her friends. "That umbrella roof is impressive."

"We're sorry we didn't help you before," Camille says.

"That's okay," Kendall replies. "You guys came through in the end. But the fort is still missing something."

"What?" her friends ask.

"Decorations!" Kendall says.
The WellieWishers add the perfect decorations to make the snow fort cozy for their animal friends.

They finish just in time! The storm clouds are close now.

The animals come by a few minutes later. They snuggle right in.

"Aw!" says Ashlyn. "They love it!"

"The fort was a great idea, Kendall," Camille says.

The other WellieWishers agree.

Kendall smiles. "It was a great idea, but it turned out even better because we all did it together."

Turn the page
for a paper doll of
Kendall!

Kendall™

Safety first!
When you see this symbol, be sure
to ask an adult to work with you.

To dress your Kendall paper doll:

1. Ask an adult to help you carefully cut out the clothing
   and accessories. Be sure to cut along all solid black lines,
   including slots.

2. Fold the tabs on the dotted lines and attach the clothing and
   accessories to your paper doll. Some tabs have slots to connect
   them together to help the clothes stay on better.

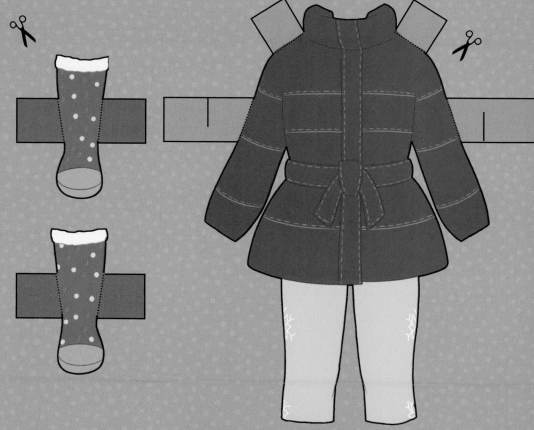

The tabs on Kendalls's play pieces can be folded back along the dotted lines to allow the items to stand up.

Want more clothes for Kendall?

1. Use the cut-out clothes as stencils to trace blank clothes on paper.

2. Use colored pencils, markers, or even glitter and stickers to design your own outfits!

3. Ask an adult to help you cut out the clothes. Don't forget to leave tabs!